Amy Wild, Animal Talker

The Musical Mouse

Diana Kimpton

Illustrated by
Desideria Gui

USBORNE

The Clamerkin Clan

Hilton

Amy

Einstein

Plato

Isambard

Bun

Willow

To Brogan

First published in the UK in 2009 by Usborne Publishing Ltd., Usborne House, 83-85 Saffron Hill, London EC1N 8RT, England. www.usborne.com

Text copyright © Diana Kimpton, 2009

Illustration copyright © Usborne Publishing Ltd., 2009

The right of Diana Kimpton to be identified as the author of this work has been asserted by her in accordance with the Copyright, Designs and Patents Act, 1988.

Cover photograph © Warren Photographic

The name Usborne and the devices ♀ ⊕ are Trade Marks of Usborne Publishing Ltd.

A CIP catalogue record for this book is available from the British Library.

First published in America in 2012 AE.

PB ISBN 9780794531454 ALB ISBN 9781601302687

JF AMJJASOND/12 00074/1

Printed in Dongguan, Guangdong, China.

CHAPTER ONE

"I wish I could stay at home with you," said Amy Wild, as she pushed her pencil case into her bag.

"Sorry – that's not possible," squawked the parrot perched in front of the TV. "Going to school is part of being human."

"Plato's right," barked Hilton. The cairn terrier jumped up on the sofa and nuzzled Amy's hand. "Don't worry. You'll be fine."

Amy wasn't surprised to hear the dog and the parrot speak. It was only a week since she had moved to Clamerkin Island, but she was already used to being the only human who could talk to animals – thanks to the magic necklace she'd been given. She was less relaxed about what the future held in store for her this morning. "It's easy for you two. You don't have to go to a brand-new school where you don't know anyone."

"You know Einstein," said Plato. "He's promised to keep an eye on you and tell you where everything is."

That made Amy feel better. Einstein
was one of her new Island friends. He
was also the school cat.

Suddenly, she heard Mom calling. "Are
you ready, sweetheart? It's time to go."

Amy ran out into the hall, with Hilton trotting at her heels. Then she stepped through the swinging door that separated the private part of her new home from the public area.

The Primrose Tea Room wasn't open for business at the moment. The counters, tables and chairs were covered with dust sheets, and Dad was hard at work painting the ceiling. When he saw Amy, he put down his roller and waved. "Let's have a look at you," he called from the top of the stepladder.

Amy spun around to show off her school clothes. The white shirt and gray skirt felt stiff with newness. But the blue sweatshirt didn't. It was soft and comfortable.

"Very nice," said Dad.

Mom nodded approvingly, too. Then she frowned and pointed at the chain of golden paws hanging around Amy's neck. "You shouldn't wear jewelry to school."

"But Granty gave it to me," argued Amy.

"That was very kind of your great-aunt," said Mom. "But it doesn't change the situation. You'll have to take the necklace off."

Amy definitely didn't want to do that. But she knew she would never persuade Mom to change her mind. "I'll put it in my room," she called, as she raced upstairs.

Hilton ran beside her. "You can't

leave it behind. You need it."

"I know," said Amy. The necklace of paws was magic. It gave her the power to talk to animals, but only when she was wearing it. If she took it off, she wouldn't be able to understand anything Einstein said to her at school.

She stopped in front of the mirror on the landing and tucked the necklace carefully inside her shirt. Then she crouched down in front of Hilton and asked, "Can you see it?"

"Not a glimmer," replied the terrier, wagging his tail.

Mom didn't spot it either. "Good girl," she said, when she saw Amy's apparently bare neck. "Now we'd better hurry or you'll be late."

"Good luck," Dad called from the stepladder. "I'm sure you'll love it."

Amy felt less confident as she followed Mom out of the front door and down the cobbled street. Tomorrow she would walk to school by herself like the other children of her age. But Mom

had insisted on going with
her on her first day.

A Siamese cat
trotted over to
them from the
post office.
"Don't worry," she
mewed. "Einstein's waiting for you."

Amy crouched down and stroked the
cat's head. "Thanks, Willow," she
whispered quietly so that only the cat
could hear.

"Stop dawdling," said Mom. "I don't
know what's gotten into you since we
came to the Island. You seem to spend
more time with animals than you do
with people."

Amy knew the reason, but she

couldn't tell Mom. As she ran to catch up, she put her hand to her throat and felt the necklace safe in its hiding place. She knew its magic powers had to stay secret. Granty had told her so. If they didn't, someone might try to misuse them.

Amy and Mom turned right onto a narrow, twisty lane and heard the school before they saw it. The sound of children playing was unmistakable. Then a bell rang out and the chattering voices died away.

"We're just in time," said Mom, as they rounded the last bend and saw the school in front of them. It was built of the same honey-colored stone as all the other buildings on the Island. So was the wall that surrounded it. A large oak tree stood in the middle of the playground, and the children were lining up beside it, ready to go into class.

Amy's stomach knotted with fear. She tried to swallow, but her mouth had gone dry. If only she was somewhere else – anywhere but this strange place full of strange faces.

CHAPTER TWO

As Amy walked nervously through the school gate, a white Persian cat jumped down from the school wall. He ran toward her and rubbed himself against her legs. "Don't look so scared," he purred. "No one's going to eat you."

Amy felt more confident with
Einstein beside her. "I'm glad you're
here," she said, forgetting that Mom
could hear her.

Luckily, Mom assumed Amy was
talking to her. "It's good to know I'm
appreciated," she said.

A plump, middle-aged woman
hurried over to greet them. Her skirt
flapped around her legs as she walked.
"You must be Mrs. Wild," she said, as
she shook Mom's hand. Then she
turned to Amy and smiled. "I'm Mrs.
Damson – your new teacher. You'd
better come with me."

Amy looked around curiously as she
and Mom followed Mrs. Damson
through the main door. Her old school

in the city was large and modern with over three hundred students. This one had a cozy, old-fashioned feel, and it was much, much smaller.

Mrs. Damson took Mom into the office and left her to sort out the paperwork with Mr. Plimstone, the principal. Then she strode off down the corridor so fast that Amy had to hurry to keep up. Einstein bounded along beside her, naming the doors that they passed. "Staffroom, bathrooms, kindergarten, gym..."

But Amy couldn't concentrate on the names. She was too worried about meeting her new class for the first time.

She didn't have to wait long. Mrs. Damson stopped beside the last door

down the hall and pushed it open.
"This is your class," whispered
Einstein, as they stepped into the
room. The children inside instantly
stopped talking and stared at Amy.
There were fifteen of them altogether
– eight girls and seven boys.

Amy's spine tingled with fear. She
decided it was best not to stare back
at the other children. So she looked
around at her new surroundings
instead. The classroom was a strange
mix of old and new. The high windows
and wooden desks reminded her of
pictures she had seen in history books.
But the whiteboard was modern and
so was the line of computers along the
far wall.

"This is Amy," Mrs. Damson announced. Then she made everyone in the class stand up one at a time and introduce themselves.

Amy tried really hard to remember who was who. But it was difficult, especially with Jade and Josie Tink. The twins were so identical that they even giggled in the same way.

Mrs. Damson waited until Amy was settled at an empty desk. Then she quickly moved on to the first lesson.

"I hope it's a story," purred Einstein, as he curled up under Amy's chair.

But it wasn't. It was math. That disappointed the white cat, but it pleased Amy. She flew through her worksheet faster than anyone else and was soon moved on to a much harder one. Her success boosted her confidence. Unfortunately, it also caused problems.

"Show-off," muttered Veronica Runcorn as they went out for recess. She glared at Amy and added, "We don't like show-offs here."

Amy stepped backward, away from her accuser. "But I wasn't—"

"We don't like overners, either," growled Nathan Ballad, without giving her time to finish. He poked her with a finger and chanted, "Overner, overner, overner."

Although Amy had no idea what the word meant, she could tell it wasn't anything good. Tears pricked her eyes as he prodded and insulted her, but she didn't want to give her tormentor the satisfaction of seeing her cry. So she spun on her heel, put her nose in the air and marched off across the playground with Einstein at her side.

She hoped one of the other children would come after her. But they didn't. Although they hadn't joined in with Nathan's taunts, they hadn't stood up to him either.

Amy had to stop when she reached the wall. She stood and stared at it with her arms folded across her chest. "No one likes me," she grumbled, as she scuffed one foot back and forth across the ground.

"I do," said Einstein. He rubbed against her legs and purred. "So will the others when they get to know you. Veronica's only upset because she's usually best at math. And Nathan's just being awful, as usual. He's somewhat of a bully."

"I'd noticed," said Amy. "What is an overner anyway?"

"Someone who comes from off the Island. From 'over the water', you see? But it's no big deal. I'm an overner too. I came from the mainland when I was just a kitten."

Amy bent down and tickled him in his favorite spot behind his left ear. "I'm glad you did. I'd hate it at school without you."

They went on talking until the bell rang for the end of the morning recess. Amy held back from the other children and joined the end of the line, well away from Nathan. When they had filed back into the classroom, Mrs. Damson opened the lid of the piano and sat down on the stool, ready to play.

"It's singing," purred Einstein. "That's almost as good as a story." He lay down happily under Amy's chair, ready to listen.

Amy was happy about the music class too. She liked music even more than math. But she was careful not to sing too loud. She didn't want to be accused of showing off again.

They were halfway through the first song when she heard another voice join in. Someone was singing much higher than everyone else — much higher than any human voice could reach.

CHAPTER THREE

Amy looked around the classroom.
No one else seemed to have noticed
the new voice, and there was no sign
of its owner.

Suddenly, Jade and Josie Tink
jumped to their feet. They pointed
at the whiteboard and screamed,
"Mouse!"

The class exploded in an uproar as

everyone tried to see what the twins were looking at. Amy spotted the mouse as he scurried for cover. But Mrs. Damson didn't turn around fast enough. By the time she looked at the whiteboard, even the tip of his tail had disappeared.

"There's no mouse there," she insisted. She clapped her hands for silence and frowned at Jade and Josie. "Sit down, both of you, and don't make up any more stories." She waited until the class had calmed down. Then she started playing the piano again.

Amy sang along with everyone else. At first, everything seemed normal. Then she heard the high-pitched voice again. She immediately looked at the whiteboard, but the singer wasn't there.

"Mouse," squealed Veronica Runcorn, pointing at a shelf. As the class erupted again, Amy saw the mouse jump behind some books. Judging by the amount of squealing 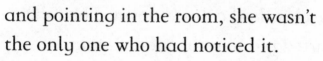 and pointing in the room, she wasn't the only one who had noticed it.

Once again, Mrs. Damson was too slow. By the time she turned around, the uninvited singer was nowhere to be seen. "There is NO MOUSE," she declared even more firmly than before. "Now stop this nonsense, all of you. If there's any more silliness, you will all have to stay in at lunchtime." She bent her head over the keys and started to play again.

Amy didn't want to trigger that punishment. It would make her even more unpopular than she already was. So she kept very quiet when she saw the mouse appear again. This time he was on top of the piano, above Mrs. Damson's line of vision. He was balancing on his back legs while he waved his front feet in time with the music.

Amy could hear him singing beautifully in his high-pitched voice, but she knew no one else would be able to. Without the magic necklace to help them, the most they would hear would be a few squeaks.

One by one, the other children spotted the mouse. But Mrs. Damson's threat was so effective that none of them said anything about him. They just stared and stared and gradually stopped singing.

When Mrs. Damson looked up from the keyboard to find out what had gone wrong, she found herself face-to-face with the small, furry visitor on top of the piano. "Mouse!" she screamed, as she jumped onto the stool. She pulled her skirt tight around her knees and screamed again.

Assuming it was now safe to join in, the class screamed with her. "Mouse, mouse, mouse!" they yelled. Only Amy stayed quiet. The tiny creature had fled behind a pile of magazines in terror. She didn't want to scare it anymore.

Suddenly, the classroom door slammed open. "What's going on here?" roared Mr. Plimstone, as he stormed into the room. He glared at Mrs. Damson, who was still standing on the stool. "That is not a dignified way for a teacher to behave."

Mrs. Damson climbed nervously to the ground, still holding her skirt close to her legs. "There was a mouse," she twittered. "On the piano."

"And on the shelf," added Veronica.

"And on the whiteboard," said Jade and Josie, in unison.

"Nonsense," said Mr. Plimstone. "We can't possibly have a mouse. We have a cat."

"Then he's not doing his job very well," said Mrs. Damson. "I assure you there was a mouse. I saw it myself, and it was this big." She held her hands out to indicate a size more suitable for a well-fed rat.

Mr. Plimstone raised his eyebrows in disbelief, but didn't comment. "Where's that cat?" he asked.

"He's under there," said Jade, pointing at Amy's chair.

"He likes the new girl," added Josie.

"Talk about bad taste," Nathan sneered at Amy, too quietly for either of the teachers to hear.

"Oops!" Einstein cried, as everyone looked at him. "Time I left." He sprang to his feet and made a run for the door. But he wasn't quick enough. Mr. Plimstone caught him by the scruff of his neck.

The principal tucked the white cat under his arm and marched over to the piano. He peered closely at the top, poking and prying among the junk that had been dumped there. At first, he found nothing. Then he pushed the pile of magazines out of the way and revealed the very surprised mouse that was hiding behind it.

The whole class squealed and rushed forward for a better look. Mrs. Damson didn't tell them to go back to their chairs — she was too busy jumping back onto the stool. Only Mr.

Plimstone stayed calm. "Catch that mouse," he ordered, as he dumped Einstein onto the piano top.

The mouse took one look at the cat and fled down the small gap behind the piano. To Amy's surprise, Einstein made no attempt to stop him.

"What are you waiting for?" yelled Mr. Plimstone. He heaved the piano away from the wall, and pushed Einstein into the gap. "Catch that mouse," he commanded.

Einstein waved his tail angrily. But Amy was too far away to tell whether he was cross with the mouse or the principal. She squeezed between Josie and Veronica to get a better look and reached the front just as Einstein backed out of the gap without the mouse.

"Failed again!" declared Mr. Plimstone. "You really are a useless cat."

Einstein hung his head in shame and crept over to Amy.

She couldn't bear to see her friend so miserable. "It's not his fault," she said, pointing at a mousehole behind the piano. "The mouse must have gotten away before Einstein had a chance to catch him."

But Mr. Plimstone wasn't accepting any excuses. "There wouldn't be a mouse at all if that cat was doing its job right. If he doesn't deal with it soon, that cat will have to go."

Amy stared at him in horror. She couldn't bear the thought of losing her only friend at school. And she couldn't understand why Einstein hadn't chased the mouse. What on earth was wrong and was there anything she could do to help?

CHAPTER FOUR

Amy found it hard to concentrate on her schoolwork for the rest of the morning. She was too busy worrying about the mouse problem. She was still thinking about it when the lunch bell rang.

"Everyone eats their sandwiches in the gym," said Einstein, as the rest of the class rushed out of the room.

Amy followed behind, glad she had the cat for company.

But Mrs. Damson grabbed Einstein as he tried to follow Amy into the gym. "He's not allowed near the food," she explained as she shut him outside.

That left Amy alone. By the time she found her class's table, it was almost full. To her dismay, the only empty chair was directly opposite Veronica Runcorn.

"I'm sorry I upset you," Amy said as she sat down.

"So am I," replied Veronica. Then she turned away and started chatting with Jade and Josie as if Amy wasn't there.

Amy tried not to show she was upset. She concentrated hard on her egg and tomato sandwiches and her slice of Granty's homemade banana cake. But she felt very lonely. *This is what it will be like all the time if Einstein goes*, she thought. *There must be something I can do to keep that from happening.*

As soon as she'd finished eating, she followed the other children onto the playground and found the white cat waiting for her in a quiet spot by the wall. It was a good place to talk – no one would overhear them there.

Einstein looked as miserable as she felt. "I don't want Mr. Plimstone to send me away," he mewed.

"Then catch the mouse."

"I can't," groaned Einstein. "I don't know how."

Amy smiled. So that was the problem. And it sounded an easy one to solve. "I'm sure the clan can sort that out," she said. They were the group of animals that looked after Clamerkin and Amy was the only human member. "As soon as I get home from school, I'll ask Hilton to call a meeting."

The shadows were growing long as Amy and Hilton ran down the Primrose's yard to the clump of bushes at the end. They squeezed between the branches until they reached the grassy patch in the middle that was the clan's almost-secret meeting place.

Most of the other clan members were already there. As usual, Plato had

stayed at home to watch TV. But
Willow, the Siamese cat from the post
office, was sitting on the grass washing
her tail. Beside her lay Bun, the fat

black cat from the bakery, and a rather grubby tabby named Isambard, who lived at the local repair shop.

Einstein was the last to arrive. He slunk into the clearing with his head hung low. He looked even more miserable than when Amy had left him at the end of school. "It's gotten worse," he moaned. "Mr. Plimstone has decided that I'm not hunting because I'm not hungry enough. He says he won't give me any more food until I've caught that mouse."

Bun's eyes opened wide in horror. "No food! That's terrible. You'll have to catch it."

"I don't know how," Einstein wailed.

Isambard's eyes opened wide in

amazement. "But you're a cat. That's what cats do. Didn't your mother teach you anything?"

"She showed me how to rub myself against people's legs and purr. That's all I've needed until now."

"Can't the rest of you teach him?" asked Amy.

"Count me out," said Hilton. "I know as little about mouse-hunting as he does."

"But I'm quite an expert," said Isambard. "Bun! Pretend to be a mouse!"

The fat cat groaned. "Why do I always get the rotten jobs?" But he did as he was told and sat down in the middle of the clearing. "Squeak! Squeak!" he said in a very unconvincing imitation of a mouse.

"Now creep up behind him," ordered Isambard. "No, not like that. He'll hear you coming. You have to be quiet. Paddy feet."

"And don't breathe so loud," said Willow. "You'll scare him away."

Amy was impressed by how hard Einstein was trying. His feet made almost no sound on the grass, and his breathing was so gentle that she was worried he'd pass out from lack of air. Eventually he reached a point just a few inches from the squeaking black cat.

"Crouch down," Isambard ordered. "Lower, lower. Now wiggle your bottom from side to side to get your balance."

"What for?" asked Einstein.

"So you can leap on his back and bite him hard on the neck."

Bun stopped squeaking and jumped into the middle of a nearby bush. "You didn't say anything about him biting me," he grumbled, as he peered out between the leaves.

"Maybe he could do it gently," suggested Amy, hoping he could be equally kind to the real mouse.

"Maybe he couldn't," said Bun. "I'm not finding out."

Isambard looked at Willow. "You'll have to be the mouse instead."

"No way!" said the Siamese cat. She pointed a paw at a flower just in front of Einstein. "Pretend that dandelion's a mouse, instead."

"I suppose that will have to do," said Isambard. He turned back to Einstein and ordered, "Jump onto the mouse and bite it really hard."

"But that's not kind," said Einstein.

"Of course it's not kind," roared Isambard. "You are a cat. You're not supposed to be kind to a mouse. You're supposed to kill it."

Einstein stepped back in horror. "I can't kill him. He likes music."

"And he's got a beautiful singing voice," added Amy, who was equally appalled at the idea of killing the mouse.

Isambard lay down on the grass, put his paws on his head and groaned. "I give up. You take over his education, Willow."

The Siamese cat stood up with her head high and her tail stuck straight up in the air. "Listen carefully, Einstein," she said in a very teacherly voice. "Cats catch mice. It's what we do. It's the reason we have sharp teeth and claws."

"I don't care," said Einstein, who seemed close to tears. "I really don't want to leave here. But I'd rather be

sent away to the Cats' Home than hurt such a musical mouse."

Amy was proud of him. It took courage to risk his own future in order to be kind. If only there was some way to save him.

Then she had an idea. "Come on, Hilton," she called, as she waved goodbye to the others. "We've got to talk to that mouse."

CHAPTER FIVE

Amy raced up the yard with the terrier bounding beside her. She paused by the open kitchen window and called, "I'm just going for a walk with Hilton."

Granty looked up from the saucepan she was stirring and smiled. "Don't be long. Supper's almost ready."

Amy promised not to be late. Then she and Hilton ran as fast as they could down the street and along the lane to the school. There were no children there now. The whole place looked deserted and the gate was firmly closed.

"What do we do now?" asked Hilton, as he peered into the playground. "You'll be in big trouble if you're caught in there without permission."

Amy scratched her nose thoughtfully. "If we can't get to the mouse, we'll have to persuade the mouse to come to us." She led the way around the outside of the wall until she was as close as she could get to the school building. Then she started to sing the song Mrs. Damson had played in music class.

Hilton tipped back his head and

started to howl along with her. His
singing was dreadful. It was completely
out of tune.

"Shh!" said Amy. "I think it's better
if I do it by myself."

Hilton's ears drooped in disappointment.
"I was only trying to help," he muttered.

"I know," said Amy, as she tickled him under his chin. "Can you help me spot the mouse instead? You've got much sharper eyes than me."

The dog instantly cheered up. He stared importantly at the wall, while Amy started to sing again. Nothing happened during the first verse. Nothing happened during the second. Hilton started to get restless. "Is this going to work?" he asked.

"I hope so," said Amy, who was starting to get anxious herself. She took a deep breath and started singing the third verse. After only a few words, she heard a familiar high voice join in with her. She forced back the urge to squeal with delight as she looked around for the mouse. Now she had found him, she didn't want to scare him away.

Hilton spotted him first. "He's over there," he whispered, nodding his head in the direction of the mouse. He was perched on top of the wall about a yard away.

Amy gave him a tiny wave. "You sing very well."

The mouse looked surprised. "Most humans just think I'm squeaking."

"I don't," said Amy. She pulled the glittering necklace from under her shirt. "I'm the Keeper of this, so I can understand what you're saying."

"Wow!" said the mouse, as he scurried closer for a better look. "There really is a necklace of paws. I thought that legend was just a story some mouse made up long ago."

"It's real and so am I. And so is the big problem you've made for the school cat."

"Einstein will be thrown out if he doesn't catch you," Hilton explained.

"I hope you're not expecting me to help," said the mouse.

"I was sort of," Amy admitted. In fact, her whole plan depended on it.

"That's impossible. Cats kill mice. If I let him catch me, that's the end of Mozart the mouse."

"I know that," said Amy. "But he won't need to catch you if you go away. There are lots of other places on the Island where you could live, and I'll happily take you to any one you choose."

"But I don't want to go," said Mozart. "I like it here. There are so many stories and so much music. It's much better than the farm where all my friends and relatives live."

"But it must have been nice to have so much company there," said Amy. "Wouldn't you like to go back?"

"No," said Mozart. "I'm safer here. The farm cats are really fierce. But this one doesn't have a clue about catching mice."

An enormous sigh made Amy jump. She hadn't noticed Einstein creep up behind her. Neither had Hilton, and neither had the mouse. Mozart immediately scurried further away along the wall.

The white cat didn't chase him. Instead, he sat down beside Amy, with his head hung low and his ears drooping. "Even the mouse thinks I'm useless," he groaned.

"He was only telling the truth," said Hilton.

Mozart nodded. "I wasn't trying to upset you."

"You managed it anyway," said Einstein. "Maybe I deserve to be sent away."

"No, you don't," said Amy. "It's not fair to punish you for being kind." She picked up the cat and gave him a hug. "Don't worry. I'm sure we can sort this out." She tried to sound confident, but deep inside she was worried. The clan had failed and now so had her only idea. She had to find another way to save Einstein, and she had to find it fast.

CHAPTER SIX

Amy ate her supper quietly. She was too upset about Einstein to want to talk much.

"You seem miserable," said Dad, as he finished his raspberry pie.

"Is there something wrong at school?" asked Mom.

"Not really," said Amy. "There was just a little thing about a mouse.

That's all."

Mom looked horrified. "A mouse! In school? It shouldn't be allowed. Perhaps we should complain."

"Don't do that!" cried Amy. That would just make matters worse.

"Amy's right," said Granty, who had spotted her alarm. "It's not necessary. Mr. Plimstone is excellent at figuring out problems. And they do have a cat."

"At the moment," whispered Amy, so quietly that only her great-aunt could hear.

Granty winked at her to show she'd understood. Then she smiled. "I think Amy needs cheering up. Let's go to see a movie."

"Good idea," said Dad.

"But there isn't a movie theater on the Island," said Mom.

"There is tonight," explained Granty. "They're showing *Mary Poppins* at the Community Hall."

Amy had already seen that movie, but she didn't tell Granty. It was good enough to watch again, and it would be fun to go somewhere different. Although she had walked past the Hall several times, she had never been inside before.

The large, stone building was at the bottom of the hill, close to the harbor. Its wooden doors faced the sea, and tonight they stood wide open to let everyone in.

Amy and her family stepped through
them into the entrance hall and walked
up to a man sitting behind a small
table.

"Three adults and a child, please,

Bill," said Granty, as she gave him some money.

Bill sneezed loudly. "Nice to see you," he said. Then he smiled at Amy. "Is this your great-niece you were telling me about?"

"That's right," said Granty.

Bill sneezed three more times in swift succession. "You've been playing with cats, haven't you."

Amy stared at him in surprise. "How do you know?"

Bill sneezed again and laughed. "I'm so allergic to them that just a few hairs on your clothes is enough to set me off. It's a shame really. I'd like to have a cat here to keep me company. But it's impossible."

Granty took their tickets and led the way into the main hall. It wasn't like any theater Amy had ever been to before. It had stone walls and a high, beamed roof. Wooden chairs stood in lines facing the stage at one end, and a huge, white screen hung down from the roof above the stage.

Almost all the chairs were already taken, but they managed to find some empty ones just in time. As they sat down, Bill turned out the lights. The buzz of conversation died away and the movie began.

Amy loved the story, and she knew the songs so well that she had to force herself not to sing along with them. That reminded her of Mozart, and *that* gave her a glimmer of an idea.

"Do they have movies in the Community Hall every night?" she asked on the way home.

"No," Granty replied. "But there's almost always something going on. Plays, concerts, that sort of thing. Even if there's not an actual show, there's usually someone rehearsing."

"I thought I might join the choir," said Mom. "There was a notice saying they practice in the Hall every Wednesday."

Music and stories, thought Amy. And no cats. The Community Hall seemed to be the perfect home for a musical mouse. But would Mozart be willing to move?

*

Amy was so eager to find out that she went to school extra early the next morning. When she arrived, she saw a blue plastic box beside the front door. It had a handle on the top and metal bars at the front.

"It's a cat carrier," said Einstein. His voice shook a little, as if he was about to cry. "I've got until the end of school to catch the mouse. If I haven't, Mr. Plimstone's sending me to the Cats' Home on the five o'clock boat."

"I'm not going to let that happen," Amy promised, as she tickled him behind his ears. Einstein listened carefully while she told him all about the Community Hall and her plan to move Mozart. Then they set off together to find the mouse.

But they couldn't. There was no sign of Mozart before school, and no sign of him during morning recess. "Maybe he's gone away," said Amy.

Mrs. Damson suspected that too. "I don't think the mouse is here anymore," she told Mr. Plimstone when he came into the classroom before lunch. "Maybe the cat has already caught him."

"I don't think so," said Mr. Plimstone. "There's no sign of a dead mouse around the school — not even a tail."

He spotted Einstein hiding under Amy's desk and strode across the room toward him. Amy felt the cat shrink back against her legs as the principal approached. But it didn't do any good.

Mr. Plimstone pulled Einstein out and glared at him. "This is your last warning, cat. I want to see a dead mouse by the end of the day or you're going to the Cats' Home."

Amy gulped. Just moving Mozart to the Community Hall wouldn't solve the problem anymore. But she didn't want to kill the mouse and neither did Einstein. Time was running out for the white cat, and it looked as if nothing could save him now.

CHAPTER SEVEN

Amy and Einstein didn't bother to look
for Mozart at lunchtime. There didn't
seem any point. But as they walked around
the edge of the playground, they heard a
squeaky voice roar, "Fee fie fo fum!"

They found the mouse behind a trash
can. He was standing on tiptoe with
his hair fluffed out to make himself
look bigger.

"Fee fie foe fum!" he squeaked again when he saw they were watching. "Look at me. I'm a giant."

"No, you're not," said Einstein. "You're a mouse."

"I know," said Mozart. "But I am a mouse pretending to be a giant. I'm acting out the story I heard this morning in the kindergarten class."

"So that's where you were," said Amy. "We've been looking for you everywhere."

Mozart twitched his whiskers in alarm. "What for?"

"I'm supposed to kill you," said Einstein. "But don't worry," he added, as Mozart retreated to a safe distance. "I'm not going to." He rolled on his back and waved his feet in the air to show he wasn't a threat.

Mozart crept closer again. "So why are you looking for me?"

"To ask you to move," said Amy.

"I don't want to. I've already told you that."

"But you might now, because I've found you somewhere even better to live. The Community Hall has much more going on in it than the school. There are movies and concerts and plays."

"Plays!" shrieked Mozart, jumping up and down in excitement. "That's real acting — not just pretending. Do you think they might have a part for a mouse?"

"No," said Amy firmly. "It would be best if no one there ever sees you."

"It would have been better for me if no one *here* had ever seen you," said Einstein. He gave a huge sigh. "Even if you move, I'll still have to go to the Cats' Home."

"Why?" asked Mozart. "You'll have gotten rid of me."

"But not in the way that Mr. Plimstone wants. I've got to show him your dead body or I've got to go." He sighed again.

So did Amy. Then she smiled. "How good are you at acting?" she asked Mozart.

"Excellent! Fantastic! Superb!" declared the mouse.

"But not modest," whispered Einstein.

"Shush!" Amy whispered back. "I've thought of something that might save you, but we can't do it without his help." Then she asked Mozart, "Can you play dead?"

"Aargh!" shrieked Mozart at the top of his tiny voice. He put one paw to his throat and staggered  sideways. Then he groaned loudly and staggered the other way. Finally, he collapsed onto his stomach with all four legs outstretched, gave a huge gasp and closed his eyes.

"Is he all right?" asked Einstein.

"I hope so," said Amy.

Mozart opened his eyes and winked. "How's that for acting?"

"Very convincing," said Einstein.

"But a little overdramatic," said Amy. "We don't need a big death scene like that. You just need to play dead long enough to fool Mr. Plimstone."

"You'll have to be really convincing," said Einstein.

"No problem," said the mouse. He slumped to the ground and lay completely still.

Amy was impressed. But there was still one more thing she had to test. "Pick him up," she told Einstein.

Mozart's eyes snapped open and looked straight into the cat's open mouth. "Be careful with those teeth."

Einstein grinned. "Don't worry. You won't feel a thing. Now go back to being dead."

"And be quiet," warned Amy. "This is a non-squeaking part."

Mozart shut his eyes again and stayed absolutely still as the cat picked him up. He hung limply from his mouth and didn't even grunt when Einstein put him down at Amy's feet.

Amy burst into applause. That was a mistake. The mouse jumped to his feet, balanced on his back legs and bowed.

"Don't do that in front of Mr.
Plimstone!" warned Amy. "You must
stay dead until no one can see you."

At that moment, the bell rang for
the end of lunch. There was no time for
more practices now. The next time she
saw Einstein and the mouse they would
be doing their performance for real.

"Bring Mozart into the classroom," she told the cat. "Mr. Plimstone is sure to come running when he hears Mrs. Damson scream."

It felt strange to go back to the classroom without the cat. She wasn't the only one who noticed he wasn't there.

"Where's your furry friend?" sneered Nathan. "Is he hiding to avoid being sent away?"

"I hope he is," said Jade.

"So do I," said Josie. "I don't want him to go."

Nathan gave an unpleasant laugh. "He's got no chance of staying. He's too much of a scaredy-cat to catch a mouse."

The conversation was cut short by the arrival of Mrs. Damson. She shut the door behind her and started the class. In other circumstances, Amy would have enjoyed learning about the history of the Island. But she found it hard to pay attention. She was too busy waiting for Einstein to arrive.

The hands on the classroom clock ticked slowly around. But there was still no sign of the cat. Amy fidgeted anxiously in her seat. If they didn't get here soon, it would be too late.

For the final part of the class, Mrs. Damson called Nathan and Veronica out to the front. She helped them put on old-fashioned clothes to show how people would have looked three hundred years ago. Nathan loved being the center of attention. He waved his fake sword and pretended to kill an imaginary dragon.

The rest of the class were so busy watching that only Amy heard the gentle tap on the window next to her. She turned and saw Einstein balanced on the outside windowsill. He was alone – there was no sign of Mozart. The cat put his mouth close to the glass and said, "I can't get in."

Amy glanced around and saw that he was right. Mrs. Damson had closed the door, and all the windows were shut too. Unless Amy did something fast, the whole plan was going to fail. So she lifted the catch and pushed the window open.

"Help!" screeched Einstein, as it banged into him. He scrabbled desperately to save himself. But his claws

couldn't get any grip on the concrete
sill. With a plaintive mew, he slid off
the edge and disappeared from sight.

Amy jumped up in alarm and put
her head out of the window. She
breathed a sigh of relief when she saw

Einstein below her, completely unhurt. Mozart was there too, standing close beside the white cat.

Suddenly, she heard a voice behind her. "What exactly are you doing, young lady?" asked Mrs. Damson.

Amy quickly pulled her head back into the room. Then she spun around and realized everyone was staring at her. "Nothing," she lied. "I just felt a little hot and needed some air."

"You've had plenty of that by now," said Mrs. Damson. "Kindly close that window."

Reluctantly, Amy leaned out again to pull it shut. As she did so, she glanced down at the white cat and whispered, "It's now or never."

CHAPTER EIGHT

She had never seen Einstein move so
fast. He grabbed hold of Mozart and
sprang through the window just before
it closed. Then he landed at Amy's feet
with the mouse dangling limply from
his mouth. Mozart's acting was
fantastic – he looked completely and
utterly dead.

Mrs. Damson screamed as Einstein

ran toward her. She backed away from him toward the safety of her desk. Nathan and Veronica were already there, still wearing their old-fashioned costumes.

Veronica screamed too when she saw what the cat was carrying. Jade and Josie didn't. They cheered instead, and several of the other children started to chant, "Einstein! Einstein! Einstein!"

Just as Amy had hoped, the uproar brought Mr. Plimstone storming into the classroom. "Silence!" he roared.

In the sudden quiet that followed, Einstein marched up to the principal and carefully placed Mozart on the floor in front of him.

Amy could hardly bear to watch as Mr. Plimstone aimed a gentle kick at the small, brown body. Surely Mozart would give the game away now.

But he was an even better actor than she had realized. He didn't flinch at all as the principal's foot made contact, and he kept absolutely still as he glided across the floor.

Nathan was less controlled. He jumped backward and dropped his sword as the apparently dead mouse slid toward him. Luckily, the sword missed Mozart and landed on Nathan's toe. "Ouch!" he cried.

Mr. Plimstone ignored him. Instead, he bent down and stroked Einstein. "I'll cancel the trip to the Cats' Home," he promised. "You can have a double helping of sardines for dinner tonight."

"And some cream from me," added Mrs. Damson, as the principal strode out of the room.

Einstein rubbed happily against her legs. At the same time, he looked at Amy and mewed, "Success!"

"Places, everyone," ordered Mrs. Damson. "There's still time for you all to draw a quick picture of Veronica and Nathan."

"Shouldn't someone get rid of that first?" said Veronica, pointing at Mozart's motionless body.

"I suppose so," Mrs. Damson agreed, without enthusiasm. She took a tissue from the box on her desk to protect her fingers. Then she wrinkled her nose in disgust and reached out a shaking hand toward the mouse.

Amy held her breath. This was the part of the plan they hadn't practiced. She hoped Mozart's acting would stand up to this one final test, and she'd be able to rescue him from the trash before it was emptied.

Then Mrs. Damson's nerves got the better of her. Just as the tissue was about to touch the mouse, she pulled her hand back to her chest and cringed away from the small brown body. "Maybe this is a job for a man," she suggested.

"Don't look at me," said Nathan, as he stepped rapidly backward. He held up both hands in front of him, palms forward, in a gesture of surrender. "I don't do mice."

"Scaredy-cat!" Veronica giggled. "So much for you being a big, brave dragon-killer." Several of the other children joined in with her laughter.

Nathan folded his arms and stared

at them through narrowed eyes. "I don't notice anyone else being any braver."

"Yes, you do," said Amy with a grin. This was working out even better than she had planned. Now she had the chance of showing up Nathan at the same time as saving Mozart.

She stepped forward and gently picked up Mozart in her cupped hands.

Veronica looked at her with admiration and started to clap. Jade and Josie joined in and so did almost everyone else. Only Nathan stayed sullenly silent.

As the applause echoed around the classroom, Amy felt the mouse twitch. Her stomach knotted with fear. As fast as she could, she raised her hands to hide the movement of her lips and whispered, "Don't try to bow. If you move now, you'll spoil everything."

To her relief, Mozart went still again. But Amy knew he wouldn't be able to keep that up forever. She needed to get him away from here as quickly as she could. "I'll put it in the trash," she told Mrs. Damson.

"Thank you, my dear," said the teacher, as she held the door open for Amy. She wrinkled her nose with disgust again and added, "Don't forget to wash your hands."

Mozart stayed silent until they were right outside by the garbage cans. Then he squeaked, "You're not really going to throw me away, are you?"

"Of course not," said Amy. She slipped the mouse gently into her skirt pocket and tucked in his tail carefully so no one could see him. "Stay there and be very, very quiet."

"As quiet as a mouse," giggled Mozart.

Amy walked back into school with her hand over her pocket to make sure her passenger didn't fall out. First she went to the girls' bathroom and washed her hands with plenty of soap. When she was sure they would pass inspection by Mrs. Damson, she headed for her classroom. She arrived just as her teacher was telling everyone to go home. But Amy wasn't planning to do that right away. She still had one more task to finish before her plan was a complete success.

She grabbed her school bag and joined the rush for the gate. The lane outside was crowded with parents picking up the younger children from school. Amy wiggled between them, being careful not to squash Mozart in the crush. Then she turned down a narrow path that led toward the sea.

She was pleased to find the Community Hall wasn't locked. The front doors were slightly open, and music drifted out toward her. Someone inside was playing the piano.

"Wonderful," squeaked Mozart, as she lifted him out of her pocket. "That's one of my favorite tunes."

Amy crept quietly up the steps, slipped through the gap and put the mouse down in the entrance hall. "Bye," she said. "And don't forget to stay out of sight."

"I won't," said Mozart. "And thanks for everything. I'm going to love living here." He danced away, twirling and jumping in time with the music, until he found a gap under the baseboard.

He paused just long enough to give
Amy one final wave before he squeezed
through it.

Amy waited until the tip of his tail
disappeared. Then she walked slowly
down the steps to the seafront and

headed for home. But as she turned onto the High Street, she walked straight into Veronica Runcorn.

Amy braced herself for another nasty comment. But it didn't come. Instead, Veronica smiled at her. "Thanks for what you did at school," she said.

Amy stared at her in surprise. "It was only a mouse."

Veronica's smile grew even bigger. "It wasn't the mouse I was talking about. It was the way you stood up to Nathan. He's such a bully, and he really needed taking down a peg or two."

"I don't expect he'll like me now," said Amy. "But that won't make much difference because he didn't like me anyway."

"Neither did I," said Veronica. "But I do now and so does everyone else." She held out the brown paper bag she was carrying. "I'm sorry I've been so awful. Would you like a strawberry as a peace offering?"

"Absolutely!" said Amy. She pulled out one of the deep red fruits, bit into it and grinned. She'd only set out to save Einstein and give Mozart a new home. But in the process, she'd managed to make her first human friends on the Island. School was going to be much more fun from now on.

Amy Wild, Animal Talker

Collect all of Amy's fun, fur-filled adventures!

The Secret Necklace

Amy is thrilled to discover she can talk to animals!
But making friends is harder than she thought...

The Musical Mouse

There's a singing mouse at school! Can Amy find it
a new home before the principal catches it?

The Mystery Cat

Amy has to track down the owners of a playful orange
cat who's lost his home...and his memory.

The Furry Detectives

Things have been going missing on the Island and Amy
suspects there's an animal thief at work...

The Great Sheep Race

Will Amy train the Island's sheep in time for her
school fair's big fundraiser – a Great Sheep Race?

The Star-Struck Parrot

Amy gets to be an extra in a movie shot on the Island...
but can she help Plato the parrot land a part too?

The Lost Treasure

An ancient ring is discovered on the Island, sparking
a hunt for buried treasure...and causing chaos.

The Vanishing Cat

When one of the animals in the clan goes missing,
Amy faces her biggest mystery yet...